Next door to Little Miss Splendid's very splendid house is a castle, which has stood empty for many years.

One day, on her way to the shops, Little Miss Splendid noticed a sold sign on the castle gate.

"I wonder who has bought that?" she thought to herself.

The following day, she found out.

Little Miss Splendid was woken by a fanfare of trumpets. She looked out of the window to see three removal vans and a very splendid-looking coach and horses moving in procession up the castle drive.

A Princess had moved in next door!

At first, Little Miss Splendid was very excited.

"Living next door to a Princess must make me even more splendid," she told herself, as she walked to her dressing room.

She put on her most splendid hat and got ready to visit her new next-door neighbour. But, before she left, she stood before her magic mirror.

"Mirror, mirror, on the wall, who is the most splendid of all?" she asked the mirror.

"The Princess next door is the most splendid of all," answered the mirror.

Little Miss Splendid could not believe her ears. "But I'm the most splendid of all!"

"Not any longer," pointed out the mirror.

Little Miss Splendid watched the Princess for the rest of that week.

She looked at the Princess's splendid coach. She studied the Princess's splendid crown. And she noted the Princess's splendid robe.

Everywhere she went nobody noticed her any longer. All they talked about was the Princess and how splendid she looked.

Little Miss Splendid grew more and more jealous of the Princess.

The following week, Little Miss Splendid went shopping. She bought an incredibly ornate coach and four horses, a shimmering princess' hat and a splendidly long and flowing robe.

Little Miss Splendid was so pleased with her new purchases that she went straight into town to show them off. But no one took any notice of her.

"Good morning, Miss Splendid," said Mr Happy, without any comment on what she was wearing. "Did you hear that the Princess is coming into town later? I can't wait, it's so exciting!"

A very disappointed Little Miss Splendid went home and looked in her magic mirror.

"I do look splendid," she told herself, admiring her reflection.

But the mirror disagreed.

"The Princess next door is the most splendid of all," said the mirror. "And if I may say, you look a little ridiculous."

Little Miss Splendid was dismayed. But, what could she do?

The next morning, the answer came to her when she was reading the newspaper. The Princess had placed an advertisement for a coachman, a maid and a butler.

Little Miss Splendid smiled to herself.

A little later, she went round to see Mr Bump.

"There is a job going as the Princess's coachman," she told Mr Bump. "It would be perfect for you."

"Really?" said Mr Bump, as he accidentally broke his window.

He hurried over to the castle to apply.

Then Little Miss Splendid went to see Little Miss Scatterbrain and suggested that she applied to be the Princess's maid.

"Really?" said Little Miss Scatterbrain, rushing off to the castle as fast as she could.

Lastly, Little Miss Splendid visited Mr Muddle who was very excited at the idea of being the Princess's butler – although he took a few wrong turns before he remembered how to get to the castle!

When Little Miss Splendid saw the Princess next, it was very obvious that her three friends had got the jobs.

Mr Bump had crashed the Princess's coach and wrecked it.

Little Miss Scatterbrain had ironed the Princess's robe and burnt a large hole in it.

And Mr Muddle had muddled up the crown and the bread. He had put the bread in the safe and the Princess's crown in the oven and melted it!

The Princess did not look in the least bit splendid.

Little Miss Splendid stood in front of her magic mirror.

"Mirror, mirror, on the wall, who is the most splendid of all?" she asked.

"Little Miss Splendid is the most splendid of all," came the reluctant reply.

"I knew I was the most splendid of all!" cried Little Miss Splendid.

"Although," continued the mirror …